For Olive
(aka Small White Dog)

Text and illustrations copyright © 2016 by Gianna Marino
A Neal Porter Book
Published by Roaring Brook Press
Roaring Brook Press is a division of Holtzbrinck Publishing Holdings Limited Partnership
175 Fifth Avenue, New York, New York 10010

mackids.com

Library of Congress Cataloging-in-Publication Data

Names: Marino, Gianna, author, illustrator.
Title: A boy, a ball, and a dog / Gianna Marino.
Description: First edition. | New York : Roaring Brook Press, 2016. | "A Neal
  Porter Book." | Summary: "An adventure story about a boy and his dog
  running through the neighborhood and playing catch"– Provided by publisher.
Identifiers: LCCN 2015034419 | ISBN 9781626722873 (hardback)
Subjects: | CYAC: Dogs–Fiction. | BISAC: JUVENILE FICTION / Imagination &
  Play. | JUVENILE FICTION / Animals / Dogs. | JUVENILE FICTION / Social
  Issues / Friendship.
Classification: LCC PZ7.M33882 Bo 2016 | DDC [E]–dc23
LC record available at http://lccn.loc.gov/2015034419

Our books may be purchased in bulk for promotional, educational, or business use.
Please contact your local bookseller or the Macmillan Corporate and
Premium Sales Department at (800) 221-7945 ext. 5442 or by e-mail at
MacmillanSpecialMarkets@macmillan.com.

First edition 2016
Printed in China by Toppan Leefung Printing Ltd.,
Dongguan City, Guangdong Province

10 9 8 7 6 5 4 3 2 1

Gianna Marino

A BOY, A BALL, AND A DOG

A NEAL PORTER BOOK

Roaring Brook Press

NEW YORK

There was never a ball the boy wouldn't throw . . .

or one his dog couldn't catch.

Until one day, the wind changed.

THIS ball, the dog thought, *I might not catch.*

"**Come back!**" said the boy.

But the ball didn't listen.

"Woof!" barked the dog.

But the wind didn't listen, either.

"**WAIT!**" said the boy.

WHOOSH went the wind.

"**WOOF!**" barked the dog.

THIS ball, the dog thought, *I MUST catch*.

And he DID.

But when he turned,
the boy was nowhere to
be found.

What good was the ball without the boy?

OOOOOOOOOO

WHOOSH!

It was almost lost forever . . .

until the wind changed again.

WHOOSH! went the wind.

"**WOOF!**" barked the dog.

"YES!" said the boy.

There was never a ball the boy wouldn't throw . . .

or one his dog couldn't catch.